The Polar Bear Paddle

David Bedford
Karen Sapp

QEB
QEB Publishing

Alfie the polar bear **loved** water.

He could float quietly like a humpback whale.

He could tumble like a

blurry snowball.

And he could swim, too.
But he only ever swam in the baby pool.

Alfie could only do **the Polar Bear Paddle.**

"You're too big for the baby pool,"
said Alfie's older brothers.
"Why don't you swim in the sea with us?"
"Will you show me how?" said Alfie.

"No, we're too busy!" said Alfie's brothers,
and they swam away together.

Alfie watched Diving Bird diving in the sea.

Plop!

"Maybe Diving Bird will help me," Alfie thought.

Alfie climbed the
steps to the top of Seal's slippery slide.

"How do you swim
in the sea?"

"I
wriggle
and
squiggle!"

Alfie tried wriggling, but he felt silly.

"That's it, Alfie!" called Seal.
"Keep **squiggling!**"

But Alfie went **faster** and **faster**.

And when he reached the bottom of the slide...

Alfie flew through the air!

SPLOSH!

Alfie was in the sea!

He tried wriggling and squiggling like Seal.
He flapped his arms like Diving Bird.

But in the end he did
the Polar Bear Paddle.

When Alfie opened his eyes, he saw everyone clapping and waving!

"You were awesome, Alfie!" shouted his brothers. "Will you show us how you dive in? Please, Alfie."
"Okay," said Alfie. "I will!"

"Then **GO!**" shouted Alfie.

They **wriggled** down the slide like Seal...

"**whEEEEE!**"

They flapped through the air like Diving Bird...

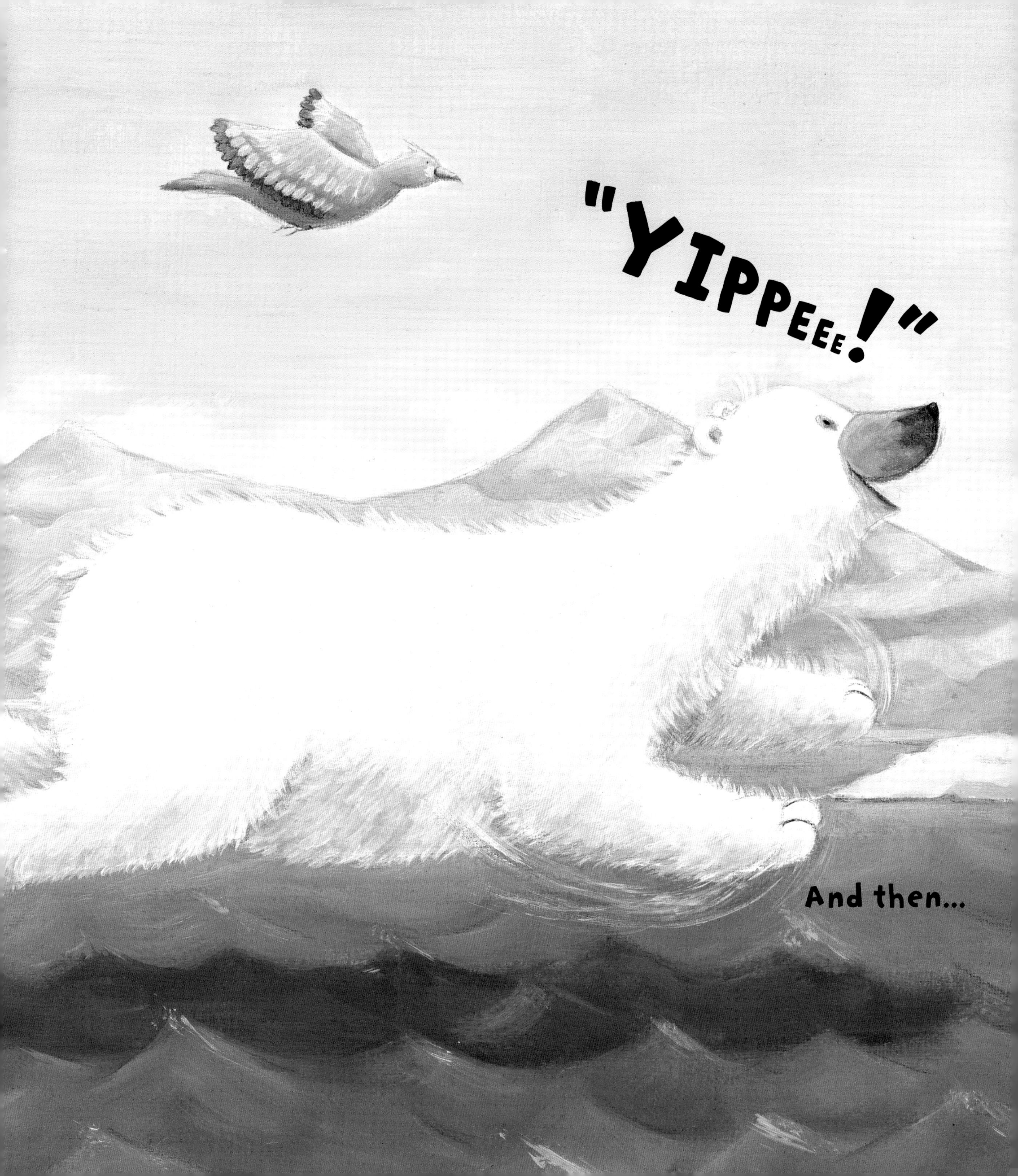

"YIPPEEE!"

And then...

After that, Alfie was happy to swim
in the sea like a polar bear.

"It's called the Polar Bear Paddle!"
Alfie told his brothers.
And he soon showed everyone how to do it!

Notes for parents and teachers

- Before you read this book to a child or children, look at the front cover and ask what they think the story is about. Then read the title.

- Read the story to the children and then ask them to read it to you, helping them with unfamiliar words and praising them for their efforts.

- Ask the children if they know where polar bears live. Discuss how the bears keep warm in very cold water, what they eat, and where their homes are.

- Do any of the children go swimming in a pool, or do they swim in the sea? Ask them to show you what they think the polar bear paddle would look like.

- Alfie was scared to go out of his baby pool. Do the children think he was brave to go swimming in the sea? Discuss with them what it means to be brave.

- Make a play of the story. One child can be Alfie, others his brothers and Diving Bird. Others can make the noises of the sea and the seal splashing through the water.

- Ask the children if they can remember who helped Alfie to swim in the sea.

- Next time the children go swimming, ask them to try doing the polar bear paddle with their arms. Talk about how this movement helps to pull them through the water.

- Ask the children to draw pictures of Alfie and the other characters in the story, using the illustrations in the book to help them. Use paints, crayons, or colored pencils to make them more colorful.

Copyright © QEB Publishing, Inc. 2009

Published in the United States by
QEB Publishing, Inc.
3 Wrigley, Suite A
Irvine, CA 92618
www.qeb-publishing.com

Library of Congress Cataloging-in-Publication Data

Bedford, David, 1969-
   The Polar Bear Paddle / by David Bedford; illustrated by Karen Sapp.
      p. cm. -- (QEB storytime)
   Summary: Alfie the polar bear loves to do the Polar Bear Paddle, but although his brothers tell him he is too old for the baby pool they are too busy to teach him how to swim in the sea and he must turn to Diving Bird and Seal for help.
   ISBN 978-1-59566-752-6 (hardcover)
   [1. Swimming--Fiction. 2. Polar bear--Fiction. 3. Seals (Animals)--Fiction. 4. Birds--Fiction. 5. Brothers--Fiction.] I. Sapp, Karen, ill. II. Title.
   PZ7.B3817995Pol 2010
   [E]--dc22

2009001997

Printed and bound in China

Author David Bedford
Illustrator Karen Sapp
Designer Alix Wood
Project Editor Heather Amery

Publisher Steve Evans
Creative Director Zeta Davies
Managing Editor Amanda Askew